THE RETURN OF

# Thelma

## THE Unicorn

· THE NEWS ·

WHERE DID THELMA GO?

?

# AARON BLABEY

Thelma felt a little shocked.
In fact, she felt quite torn.
You see, she'd made the whole world sad—

WE MISSED OUR UNICORN!

From every corner of the earth,
her fans did wail and cry—

'Thelma! Thelma! Please come back!
WHY DID YOU LEAVE US?

*WHY?!*'

Thelma's best friend, Otis
(and her all-time greatest fan),
said, 'Gee, they really miss you.
We should help them if we can . . .'

THE COUNTRY TIMES

THELMA BROKE
OUR HEARTS
WHERE IS SHE?

'Help them?' blurted Thelma.
'You mean, dress up like before?
They don't need phoney unicorns.
Of *that* I am quite sure.'

But Otis shook his shaggy head
and said, 'I think they *do*.
You're not phoney. You're the best.
And what they miss is . . .

YOU.

You made people happy.
They felt cheerful for a while.
Who cares if it's a costume?
Thelma, you made people smile.

There's nothing wrong with
make-believe.
You can be a star . . .

. . . as long as you remember what you love and *who you are.*'

'But last time it was scary.
Oh, and some of them were mean . . .'

UNICORNSAREDUMB.COM

'Well, this time you'll have backup!
I am here for you, my Queen.'

'But I don't have my outfit!
How can I disguise my face?!'

Otis said,
'I kept this.
And some glitter.
Just in case . . .'

PINK

So, just like that, they hit the road.
They barely stopped to pack.
They both had
lots of work to do . . .

S SQUARE

A IS BACK!

SHE'S BACK

THE
UNICORN
WAS
BACK!

TELEPHONE

The whole wide world was overjoyed!
Her fans all went berserk.

But this time Thelma had her friend,
and that's what made it work.

Her fabulousness exploded
like a joyful glitter bomb . . .

. . . while Otis cheered her
from the wings—
*'Girl, get your sparkle on!'*

Lives were changed . . .

MONEY RAISED FOR CHARITY

$1,500,000,000,000,000.0 ♥ Thelma

and fun was had . . .

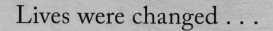

APPLAUSE

and love was in the air.

SHOWBIZ FOR DUMMIES

And at the end of every day
her friend was always there.

Otis watched her spread the love.
He felt so very proud.

STAGE DOOR

Thelma could just
*do her thing*.
He handled every crowd.

I DON'T LIKE UNICORNS

ME EITHER

So when those mean old haters
came to mock or diss or scoff,

she felt so brave and happy, she could always . . .

. . . shake it off.

And on days off, they'd cuddle up
beneath their favourite tree . . .